100%
Wisdom

100% Wisdom

By Sirshree Tejparkhi

Copyright © Tejgyan Global Foundation
All Rights Reserved 2016

Tejgyan Global Foundation is a charitable organization
with its headquarters in Pune, India.

Published by WOW Publishings Pvt. Ltd., India

First edition published in August 2016
First Reprint in November 2018

Copyrights are reserved with Tejgyan Global Foundation and publishing rights are vested exclusively with WOW Publishings Pvt. Ltd. This book is sold subject to the condition that it shall not by way of trade or otherwise, be lent, resold, hired out, or otherwise circulated without the publisher's prior written consent in any form of binding or cover other than that in which it is published and without a similar condition including this condition being imposed on the subsequent purchaser and without limiting the rights under copyright reserved above, no part of this publication may be reproduced, stored in or introduced into a retrieval system, or transmitted, in any form, or by any means, electronic, mechanical, photocopying, recording or otherwise, without the prior written permission of both the copyright owner and the above-mentioned publisher of this book. Any person who does any unauthorized act in relation to this publication may be liable to criminal prosecution and civil claims for damages.

Table of Contents

	Introduction	1
1.	The Eternal Wisdom Beyond Time	3
2.	Wisdom of the Self	13
3.	Stabilizing in Self-experience	23
4.	From Knowing to Not-knowing	32
5.	Transcending the Mind	43
6.	Discerning the Real amidst the Unreal	56
7.	The Path of Wisdom	67

Introduction

Whatever happens is not with you, but for you;
Who-you-truly-are is the pure untouched witnessing;
Know this and realize that you are freedom!

Suppose you are searching for a chocolate bar in your house. You search everywhere, in the drawing room, in the kitchen, in the bedrooms. You search every nook-and-corner; you go through every drawer and closet, but are unable to find it.

How would you feel like if you were then told that the entire house, its walls, furniture, everything… is made of chocolate!

All the time, you were in frenzy, searching the chocolate in a particular wrapper… and so, you were missing what was obvious all the time.

In the same way, the ultimate truth of life, the very essence of our existence is an open secret. It is so obvious that we easily miss it because we seek it in the wrappers of concepts and ideologies.

Truth is subjective experience, not objective knowledge. It cannot be known as you would the other topics of the world. You can only experience it by 'being' it. And to 'be' it, you need to empty your mind off concepts and notions about the Truth.

This book is part of the 'Ocean in a Drop' series. It is like the Ocean in a drop. It presents the essential wisdom of life, which has been distilled from conversations between seekers and Sirshree.

It explains the crux of true wisdom. 100% wisdom enables the seeker to start with the pure consciousness as the reference point. When people seek the Truth, in terms of concepts, they can never arrive.

With the right wisdom, one realizes that there is no need to arrive; one is already home, in one's true nature. Who-you-truly-are is already free. The notion of bondage is a myth. Freedom from this myth is true liberation!

Every answer in this book arises from the quintessence of wisdom. Scattered in these answers are 100 precious drops, which have been annotated for repeated reading (#). Reading these profound drops of wisdom and contemplating upon them can bring about a paradigm shift in the perspective of life.

1

The Eternal Wisdom Beyond Time

Seeker: Scientists theorize that the universe began from the big bang. But I keep feeling that something had to have existed before that for the big bang to occur. How did all this come about? What was there before the beginning?

Sirshree: The big bang theory suggests an explanation for the origin of the manifest universe. However, it is not difficult to sense that something has to exist prior to the big bang.

Time is a dimension that enables us to make sense of this phenomenal world; it is an essential element of the manifest universe. Time exists only when the world exists. When you question what existed 'before' time, you are trying to assume the existence of time before the existence of the world. The words 'before' and 'after' are facets of linear time. It cannot explain what exists beyond time. Consciousness – the undifferentiated state of the true Self is beyond time.

You may call it Self, or Consciousness, or God, Allah, Christ, Ishwar, or the Divine Presence. All these words point at the same living essence, which precedes the world. When one stabilises in the experience of the Self, one realizes that there is neither a 'past' nor a 'future'. The eternal present alone is. The so-called past and future are experienced in the timeless present. This is beyond the grasp of the intellect.

Let us imagine that there are some transparent photo films containing certain images. If ten such photo films are stacked together and you are asked to look at the entire stack, you will not be able to understand the images, as they overlap. You will need to keep a gap between the photographs, watch them one after the other, to understand each picture. The effect created by this gap is called 'time'.

(1) *Time is such a wondrous aspect of creation. It enables you to watch and understand the living pictures of the manifest world in sequence. Just because the element of time is brought in, the eternal 'now' gets divided into 'past', 'present' and 'future'. Time is thus a method of seeing the entire film of life in a particular sequence. Otherwise, the entire film is happening in the 'here-and-now'.*

Seeker: Thank you… that was a new perspective about time for me. If the real 'now' spans both past and future, why do I find it difficult to place my attention in the present? I always tend to be consumed by whatever has happened or what's in store.

(2) **Sirshree:** *You can either think about the present moment, or just be the present. When you attempt to capture the present moment in your thoughts, it eludes you. The mind insists, "I want to grasp the present*

moment; I want to know how it is like." This wish becomes a hurdle in just being the present.

(3) Past is memory; future is imagination. *Past and future exist merely in thoughts that arise in the timeless present. Hence, the mind has this mistaken notion that the present also can be grasped in terms of thoughts.* You experience the timeless eternal present when you see thoughts for what they truly are, without being consumed by the content of the thoughts.

(4) *The present is not an instant between the past and future that can be captured by thinking. This is the missing link that many fail to see. The Present is the space in which the past and future appear as thoughts.*

Your essential nature is Consciousness. It can be experienced as the living presence in which everything is being known. This presence is beyond time and space. The world appears like waves on the surface of the ocean of pure silence. All forms and phenomena arise and dissolve in this eternal silence. Even thoughts are like waves that arise from and dissolve into this knowing presence.

This Consciousness, which is the real Self, pervades all manifestation. It is the living screen of consciousness on which the movie of life is being projected. This screen is the creator, the projector and also the experiencer of the movie of life.

Seeker: What is the purpose of all this? Why did God create this world? Wasn't He happy without creating it?

Sirshree: When a nightingale sings, would you ask why it 'needs' to sing? No. Singing is not the nightingale's need; it is its nature. It's only man who assesses everything in terms of needs and benefits. Just as a bird sings, the world too is the song of God! There is no need for the word 'need'.

Have you known a painter who has never created a painting!? No. *A painter creates paintings to express himself; painting is a means for him to realize his creative potential. In the same way, the world is a painting by God, an expression of pure consciousness. The sole purpose of the world is for God to realize Himself through His creative potential.* The manifest world serves as a reflection for consciousness to be aware of itself.

Just as a painter expresses his pure unexpressed potential through his art out of sheer joy, the world too is an expression of bliss from the pure unexpressed state of God. God exists in the state of boundless bliss. When happiness is at such heights, then creation of the world is bound to happen. Every aspect of this creation is perfect as it is meant to serve the sole purpose for God to know Himself.

Seeker: If God was already in the perfect state, then what was the need to create a world that is imperfect?

Sirshree: Many people wonder why this world has been created. They question the very purpose of existence. Those who are depressed complain about life. They see this world as an imperfect place. They blame an imaginary creator for creating an imperfect world. Some go even further to the extent of concluding that it would have been better if this world were never created.

People often wonder: Why are some people deceitful, while others are noble? Why do some people sing melodiously, while others sing harshly? Why do some people appear beautiful or pleasant, while others appear ugly?

The fallacy in their questioning is not very obvious. The missing link in their understanding is a very subtle one. If the creator had never created this phenomenal world, replete with its beautiful variety, if those people who complain about imperfections were never created, how would it ever be known whether creating the world was good or bad, whether it was useful or useless? Something has to exist first in order to know how it is. If nothing existed, there would be no question of knowing!

A painter mixes the fundamental colours (red, green, blue) to create new derived colours. He creates many colours including black. One may wonder why the painter has made 'black', as it appears dark and depressing. However, for the painter, black is as important as any other colour. Thanks to black, he is able to lend depth to his art and give it a three-dimensional appearance. In some cases, black colour actually highlights and enhances the beauty of other colours by offering a contrast.

Some people sing harshly, but they are also important in the Creator's plan. If it were not for them, then those who sing melodiously wouldn't be valued. Similarly, deceit fulfils its higher purpose of elevating the value of honesty. Everything that exists has its importance. The world, in its entirety, is perfect in all its apparent imperfections. But if we look at everything from our limited perception, we will develop preferences and get into the habit of comparison and judgment.

Look at it from the creator's point of view. What is the creative intention? The sole intention behind creation is to experience and express the highest creative potential. Where there are mountains, there are bound to be deep valleys. Without the white background that pervades paper, you cannot recognize the writing in black.

Understand the cosmic game being enacted in the phenomenal world and our role in the scheme of things. When we lack the higher perspective of life, we see imperfections.

The purpose of all this is to experience your true nature. This experience can be known only by *being* that, not by *thinking about* that. Abiding in this experience and expressing its divine qualities is the ultimate purpose of human life.

Seeker: Why should this be the ultimate purpose of human life? Can't we consider any other aim and attain fulfilment?

Sirshree: Imagine a painter who paints the picture of a paintbrush. This paintbrush comes alive and serves to create more paintings *for the painter*. However, if the paintbrush *assumes* its own individual existence and a separate personal purpose, it would go about painting without consulting the painter. Though it was created to explore and manifest the painter's creative inspiration, the paintbrush will do everything else without seeking to fulfil the painter's wish – the very purpose for which it was created.

In the same way, the human body-mind mechanism is the Self's creation, which serves as an instrument or medium to manifest the *Self's* further creations. However, human beings perceive and operate individualistically instead of allowing the Self to experience and express through them. Though a lot of creations may be happening in the visible realm, they are devoid of true and lasting fulfilment, since the Self's real purpose remains unfulfilled.

Consider a sheet of paper on which letters are written. Each written letter contributes to the overall story that the author wishes to express. However, if any single letter were to decide to express itself differently, then will the story flow as the author intended? If a single letter were to look around the sheet and compare itself with the other letters, it may find some letters that are bigger, some that are *italics*, some that are **bold** and hence standout. This letter may then feel dejected by comparing thus and wish that it should be like or even better than the others.However, unless the letter attains the perspective of the author or surrenders to his will, the very purpose of why it was penned on the paper is lost.

If we draw a parallel to human life, we see that individual human life is an expression on the stage of life, contributing to the overall plan of the scriptwriter. If any person gets into the game of comparison and the need for superiority and enacts such tendencies, it becomes an abnormality, a deviation to the grand plan of the creator.

There is nothing wrong with the pursuit of other aims in life, so long as one does not remain stuck in them. Behind every human pursuit is the yearning for the experience of unconditional love, boundless joy and unbroken peace. The truth is that love, joy and peace have always been present within each one of us as the essence of our true nature. It's just that we seldom notice and experience them within.

When people lose the experience of true love, joy and peace within

them, their pursuit turns outward in the material world. Love, happiness and peace, which are qualities of who we truly are within, are invested in things of the outside world. Satisfaction in external pursuits is instant, but temporary.

Trying to find true fulfilment in external pursuits doesn't work.
(7) *In the insatiable quest to amass more and better comforts, people lose their value for true love, joy and peace. It leaves them hungry for more and so they remain dissatisfied all the time.*

It is like trying to catch the head of your shadow. It always eludes you. Catch hold of your head itself, and the shadow is automatically caught! When you seek true love, happiness and peace within, you discover their source within you – the ever-shining presence of the immaculate Self.

(8) *What you are seeking outside is like a shadow. It can never give lasting fulfilment. Your outer world only reflects your inner world. When you stabilize in the experience of Self-realization, you are one with the Source of life. You abide in the experience of the Self. Your life automatically reflects it through the expression of love, joy and peace in the external world.*

Seeker: What exactly happens with Self-realization?

Sirshree: On Self-realization, one comes to know the very first announcement with which the game of this world began. The one who forgets the first announcement gets entangled in the announcements that came later. But the day he remembers the first announcement, he remembers the purpose of life in this world. He realizes the temporary nature of the world. Self-realization is the remembering of the first announcement regarding why the world has been created.

The original state of Self is at rest when the world is not created – an unexpressed state where Self alone exists, where only subject exists. This is the state when the Experiencer is present, but cannot experience himself. This is the Self-at-Rest.

When there is only one without another, one cannot know oneself. It is only when there is 'another' that one can feel one's own presence. So as to experience Self's own presence, the Self-in-Rest brings about the state of Self-in-Action… the expression of Self. The subject creates the object, so as to experience its own presence. When Self manifests as the mind comprising thoughts, it is the state of Self-in-Action. Self experiences itself through expression.

However, when Self gets identified with the mind and body, it assumes "I am the mind, I am these thoughts, I am this body." This gives rise to an illusion of many separate bodies, many separate selves, due to an imagined sense of separateness and individuation. So, if I am 'this' body, the assumption is that I am not 'that' body, or 'those' bodies. So whatever is inside the body-skin is assumed to be 'I' and whatever is outside appears to be 'others'. However, this is merely a projection, an illusion that the Self gets entangled in. In this entanglement and false identification, the real purpose of experiencing Self's own presence is forgotten.

When Self begins to dis-identify from this illusion of separateness, inner Self-witnessing gains precedence over witnessing of the world. The ultimate purpose is realized only when there is a permanent shift from 'witnessing the world' to 'witnessing the witnessor'.

While looking at a mirror, if you do not see yourself, then the purpose of the mirror is not served. In the same way, while witnessing the world of forms and phenomena, the focus should shift to witnessing the Self. The interest should be solely transfixed on knowing the knower. The world serves as a mirror to bring awareness of the presence of the knower.

When Self-realization is attained, the conviction about non-existence or falsehood of the separate individual is established. The original nature of Self is recognized. Self continues to be in action, and yet remains dis-identified from the mind-body.

Self-realization is when the ultimate purpose of Self behind creating this world is realized… when the real-'I' is realized. The identification with an assumed separate personality, comes to an end.

Man may imagine that Self-realization is occurring within, or that he has attained Self-realization. But, when Self-realization actually happens, the individual ego-sense, which imagines this, disappears.

Thereafter, everything happening through the body is impersonal Self-expression. Thereafter, whenever thoughts arise in the body, there is no such notion that these thoughts are 'my thoughts'.

The understanding that functions in the body is: This thought has appeared because it is required for some purpose, because someone is in need of this answer. Personalized thoughts that arise in the body due to egocentric desires end automatically. The thoughts that arise are all impersonal.

2

Wisdom of the Self

Seeker: What is the nature of the Self?

Sirshree: The Self cannot be understood as one would any other subject, as it is beyond concepts, beyond the comprehension of the intellect. While it may defy explanation for many, there is no denying its existence – for it is existence itself!

While thinking and doing are the key aspects of thoughts, Being is the essence of the Self. Beingness is the experience of existence; it is the 'is-ness' of life. It's that feeling of being awake and alive, within which everything is being manifested. This experience of presence or aliveness is constantly happening within every human being.

What is it that enables your eyes to see? What is the light that enables us to see not just light, but also darkness? We may call it the Self, Consciousness, God or Source. It is the same life principle that pervades everyone and everything. It is the reason we are alive.

Awareness is the essential principle of the Self. Pure awareness, or pure wakefulness, brings about the manifestation of forms and phenomena. Our mind, comprising thoughts and feelings, is the expression of pure awareness. Our body is a dense, more obvious expression of the Self, a gross expression of the mind.

(12) *The human body-mind is a medium through which the Self experiences itself and expresses its divine qualities.* Everything is connected. Everything is the Self, alone. The Self was always there and will always continue to be. It is eternal.

Seeker: You said that our mind and body are expressions of the Self. Does this mean that the Self exists within us?

Sirshree: When you learn that the experience of the Self is constantly going on within each of us, you might imagine that this entity exists within the human body. And, though it may be considered true logically, the Self is not just within the body. Rather, the body exists within the Self.

All of this existence is happening within the Self. Supposing there are several pots in the ocean. All those pots are inside the water and there is water inside every pot. Likewise there is Consciousness inside each body and all the bodies are inside Consciousness. There is nothing other than the Self. There is only a curtain in between. The curtain stands for the identification with the body-mind. The Self is on this side of the curtain as well as on the other. There are small and large holes in the curtain. The Self is in them too.

Think of a fish living in water. Water is an all-pervading presence for the fish. It is the essential medium that keeps the fish alive. Water exists not only within the fish, but also all around it. Water is so close to its eyes that the fish doesn't realize that it's in water. What if the fish swam off in search of water, asking, "Where is water?"

This is precisely what the questioning mind would ask when it is told about the all-pervading nature of consciousness: "Where is this consciousness? Is it within me, or elsewhere?"

The experience of presence or consciousness is so close to you; in fact, it is your very essence. If you carefully observe, you will find that the spatial concepts of *within* and *outside* are relative to your body and belong in the realm of thoughts. From the standpoint of the Self, there is neither a *within* nor an *outside*. You are *presence*. Your presence is the experience of the Self.

Seeker: Why do we forget our nature? Does it have anything to do with lowered consciousness?

Sirshree: The manifest universe is the expression of the Self. The Self-in-action is like a dancer who begins to dance so fast that he cannot be clearly seen. All that is visible is the hazy expression of dance.

One will not be able to appreciate the presence of the dancer, as one is lost in the expression of dance. As one has not seen the dancer before the dance commenced, one remains stuck in the various aspects of the dance. Similarly, there is the innate tendency to forget the original state of Self-at-Rest. Awareness drifts to the expression of Self-in-Action.

When awareness is trained to return onto Self, it becomes possible to clearly spot the dancer in and through every movement of the cosmic dance. In every experience, the focus will be on the dancer —the Self-

at-Rest–without whom, the dance would not happen!

At the same time, had it not been for the cosmic dance, the dancer would not be able to recognize his infinite potential! Without this dance of the manifest universe, the dancer –Self– would not get a chance to know its own magnificent nature.

When Consciousness identifies itself as the human body-mind, it gives rise to the false notion that 'I am the body'. This is a state of the entanglement that arises from an innate tendency of forgetting one's original nature.

(14) *When the awareness of the Self for its own presence rises, then clarity is experienced. Wholeness and fulfilment are experienced at all levels – physical, mental, social and spiritual. To the extent that awareness of the Self is focused on itself, it can be said that consciousness is higher to that extent.*

(15) *When the awareness of the Self is directed towards the diverse world of forms and phenomena, it gives rise to clouding and confusion. The focus of awareness gets limited and invested in dual opposites such as joy and sorrow, pleasure and pain, life and death, love and hatred, light and darkness. To the extent that awareness of the Self moves away from itself and gets diffused in the duality of the manifest world, it can be said that consciousness is lower to that extent.*

The loss of self-awareness leads to attachment to the aspects of the manifest world. Awareness is withdrawn from the Self and gets invested in the details of the world. The wholeness of the Self is shadowed when the mind is absorbed in the objects of perception.

(16) *As a result of forgetting our essential nature, we begin to cling*

onto a false idea about our identity; an idea that is implanted by the belief-systems that we inherit through birth and upbringing of the physical body.

We become disconnected from our essential nature. Wholeness or pure consciousness – which is our true nature – is lost to us. The nature of wholeness gets fragmented and is replaced by a false illusion of separateness and limitation. This fragmentation of wholeness has a ripple effect on wellbeing at all levels of the human mind-body mechanism.

Seeker: Why does the Self need a body-mind?

Sirshree: *The experience of Self is 'Nothingness'. However, this is not the 'No-thing' that the mind may imagine. It is Nothing with the potential of everything. The Self experiences itself through the manifested world.*

Take the example of a clay pot. When the walls of the pot are made, then there is empty space inside the pot and also outside the pot. Are these two empty spaces different? No, they are one and the same.

Similarly, if we consider the walls of the pot as our body-mind, then what part of the pot do we use? Do we use the walls of the pot or the empty space inside the pot? The walls of the pot only help in realizing and using the empty space. Thus, our essence is the space and not the body.

You say that you were born on a certain date. When you realize that the empty space is the 'real I', then will you say, "I was born"? The empty space, which you essentially are, has always been present.

When you realize this, you will say, "I have not been born at all. I am unborn." If 'I' is never born, then can 'I' die? Then you are beyond birth and death. Pots will be made and broken down, but the space in which they exist lives on eternally.

(18) *The Self needs the body-mind to experience its potential, just as space needs the clay walls of the pot to realize its potential. The body-mind serves the Self in experiencing its divine presence. This presence is beyond thinking, beyond doing.*

Seeker: How can the divine presence be experienced without thinking or doing?

Sirshree: It is already being experienced every moment. It's just that you lack its recognition. The mind tries to understand it by imagining it.

A philosopher once said, "I think, therefore I am." However, if existence were dependent on thinking, then we wouldn't exist if we stopped thinking. This is certainly not the case. When we are in deep sleep, we don't think but we continue to exist. We even comment on waking that we had sound sleep. We have to exist during deep sleep to be able to know that we did sleep well.

Our essential presence is independent of thought. Presence just *is*.

Our sense of presence is the simple truth that we are constantly and spontaneously aware of. It is because we are present that we engage in all kinds of activities. "I am reading this book." "I am" comes first. It is because "I am" that "I am reading." And "I am aware that I am reading."

We tend to be lost in whatever follows 'I am...' I am a man, I am reading, I am smart, I am sad, I am an artist. Everything that follows 'I am' is subject to change. But the 'I am' is constant. It is the constant sense of presence that enlivens all activities of life.

When the judging and reasoning mind drops, the experience of conscious presence is revealed. In that state, there's neither a need to think about it nor a necessity to do anything about it.

Understand this with an example. When someone is playing the piano, rendering a beautiful symphony, he is lost when the performance is at its peak. It is as if he does not exist then. The performer is lost in the performance. All that is happening is the performance. Where is the mind when this is happening? It has dropped for some time. But the mind comes back later and claims that it was present during the performance. The mind even takes credit for having been the 'doer' of the performance.

Musicians love to be lost in the peak of their performance. Athletes like being in the thick of activity. The real joy that they experience is because the mind drops and they touch the experience of conscious presence. However, they believe that it is the music performance or the athletic activity that is giving them joy. The source of joy is not in the gross external world. True joy is the nature of your essential presence.

A clear glimpse of our true nature can awaken us from our limiting beliefs and shift us onto this enlivening presence. *Presence or 'being' is the basis of existence. Presence comes first; thinking comes next; doing comes even later. To think or do, we have to first* be. Being or Presence is our true nature. Presence is independent of thought.

Presence just *is*. It is the most obvious experience, the open secret – so open and obvious that we easily fail to notice it.

Seeker: You say that Presence just *is*. I gather that is some kind of stillness. How can it then be the basis for thinking or doing?

Sirshree: Understand this with an analogy of the ocean and waves. Each wave is essentially the movement of the ocean itself. The existence of each wave is essentially the presence of the ocean. Waves do not have an individual existence of their own… unless it is imagined to be so.

The wave is merely a form of expression of the ocean. But when the ocean identifies itself with this form of expression, it gives rise to an illusion of separateness, a notion of individuality. The wave assumes itself to be the doer.

Each human body-mind is a wave of expression of the Self. Bodies come and go, just as the waves rise and fall. But the Self, like the ocean, lives eternally and expresses incessantly through the human mechanism.

The deeper part of the ocean exists as stillness, the state of Self-at-rest. This is unexpressed and changeless, existing beneath the changing surface. The state of Self-at-rest is pure consciousness, the state of nothingness with the potential of everything.

The ocean surface is dynamic; there is movement. Waves are the dance of the ocean; they are Self-in-action. At the surface, waves arise from the deeper stillness of the ocean and die down into it. Each body-mind is like a wave; Self is like the ocean.

When the individual expressions are seen from the standpoint of the stillness of presence, they are merely an expression of this divine presence. The waves are inseparable from the ocean; the ocean is the waves and also beyond the waves. It is the mind that imagines separateness in the waves. The underlying presence sees itself through the seeing of the waves.

(22) *Know your being as the ocean, not as a wave; then you are out of the trap of mind. With true surrender, all thought and action are clearly seen as the spontaneous and passing rise and fall of waves on the surface of consciousness.*

Clarity is experienced when the mind is transcended and understood as the play of waves on the surface of the ocean of pure consciousness. The waves then serve the purpose of Self-knowing instead of assuming an individual identity.

(23) *Unconditional happiness is experienced when Presence becomes aware of itself, when "I am aware that I am", when consciousness becomes conscious of itself. This happiness is pure, independent of external factors. In fact it is the source of happiness.* When you are aware of this constant living presence, you are being aware of your pure undeniable existence. You are awake to the light that shines upon everything that is being known.

Seeker: What then is the role of thoughts?

Sirshree: Thoughts – whether they are trivial and mundane, or brilliant and revolutionary – serve merely as a medium to indicate the presence of the Self. They serve to express the divine qualities of the Self. This is the whole and sole purpose of thoughts.

Experiencing the Presence, the Self, through the medium of

thoughts can also be understood as the second news. We always focus on the first news that the content of our thoughts convey.

Suppose that a thought occurs: "It's such a lovely, bright and sunny day!" While this is the content of the thought, it is actually also conveying the news that *you are alive*. In other words, the second news is: *"I am"* or *"Consciousness exists"*. We usually get caught up with the first news and so the second essential news is lost.

As a daily practice, you can raise your awareness of the second news. You are flooded with various bits of information every minute. With every such input, you can remember the second news.

Seeker: But how can I ignore important news and just live with the truth that Consciousness exists?

Sirshree: Not at all… this does not mean that you should ignore the happenings of the world. Of course, you will heed them and take necessary action. However, everything that happens is an opportunity, an invitation, to shift to the underlying truth that the Self is enlivening all this.

There is nothing to be done to experience Presence. Thoughts may continue to occur, actions may be taken, however they need not interfere with the awareness of Presence. Presence is experienced beyond doing and non-doing.

When you abide in awareness of Presence, you go beyond the body. Bodily sensations may continue to be felt, actions may happen, but there will be a constant awareness of this formless Presence, of just being alive. The more you practice being aware of Presence, the more it will become obvious in your everyday activities.

3

Stabilizing in Self-experience

Seeker 1: Have you attained Self-realization? Are you enlightened?

Sirshree: I am… And so are you!

Jesus said, "I am the son of God. And so are you". The second sentence has rarely been given importance.

Self-realizing alone is happening. All of this existence, both collective and individual, is nothing but the Self, realizing itself.

The mind fantasizes and makes it an extraordinary attainment. It imagines Self-realization in terms of special sensory experiences such as the light of a thousand suns, divine fragrance, a primordial cosmic sound etc.

Self-realization is the most ordinary essence of life that is already happening within every being. It is who-you-truly-are. God alone exists. God alone lives through all beings. Seek and discover whether you exist or not — you, as in the limited individual that you assume yourself to be.

Seeker 1: Can I attain Self-realization?

Sirshree: Answers provided in spirituality change depending on the level of receptivity of the one who is questioning. If a beginner asks, "Can I attain Self-realization, he will be told, "Yes, you can." It is essential to open his mind to the possibility, which is his very birthright.

If someone who has progressed on the path to some extent asks the same question, he will be told, "Till today, no person has ever been Self-realized." *An assumed personality can never attain Self-realization. The 'I' that wants to attain it can never attain it. This 'I' is the mind seeking that experience. This 'I' is unreal, it's just a notion. The false 'I' can never attain it, and the real 'I' doesn't need it, for the real 'I' is constantly real-I-zing it!*

When an advanced seeker asks whether Self-realization can be attained, he will be told, "There is no question of 'attaining' Self-realization. In truth, Self-realizing alone is going on. That is the sole definitive truth of all existence." Everything that is happening is merely serving the Self to realize its own presence. The world serves as a mirror for Self-knowing.

Seeker 1: How long does this journey to Self-stabilization take?

Sirshree: Consider a student, who wakes up early in the morning and is flooded with a hurricane of thoughts: 'Today I need to submit my journal in the college . . . I have to rush to college . . . I have to reach early.' Suddenly someone tells him, 'Today is Sunday!' Having heard this, how long would it take for the storm of thoughts to die down into tranquillity? It would hardly take a moment.

Self-stabilization can be attained in the same duration. It does not take even a moment! No sooner did the student realize that it was Sunday, than all his earlier thoughts completely vanished and were replaced with new thoughts.

Similarly, if you were to realize who-you-truly-are, what would happen the very next instant? What would happen to all the thoughts that were arising out of the false identification with the body? From that state of liberation, how would you perceive all the suffering associated with the earlier set of thoughts?

This freedom can only be known through experience. Just a while ago, one might have been thinking, 'I am this hand; my hand is paining.' And now he realizes, 'I am not this hand.' How would he then regard the pain? If he is convinced that he is not the hand, that he is not the body-mind, the hand will continue to pain, but he will no longer be grieved due to the pain. This is because he has returned to the original state of pure being. Given the right understanding, it takes just a moment to attain it.

Seeker 2: When I was going around the Ashram, I was lost by the beauty of the lush green hills. It was as if I was one with everything. Is this the experience of Self-realization?

Sirshree: First, it is important to clearly understand Self-realization. It can be said that Self-realization is just the beginning. Self-stabilization is the real goal.

There are many who experience momentary flashes of oneness when they are with nature or in the midst of their daily lives. A seeker may experience a profound meditative state where he abides in conscious silence for some time. Somebody experiences oneness with everything when he is on a nature trail.

However, these are only samples of the experience of Self-realization, which appear more pronounced when the understanding of our true nature shines forth.

Self-realization is experienced only when the interfering and comparing mind disappears. But what happens after the glimpse of Self-realization? The mind emerges again and takes credit for the experience: "I performed meditation; I attained this deeply profound state; I experienced Self-realization." The mind lacks the understanding that it did not experience that state. On the contrary, when the mind was stilled, the Self experienced itself.

With Self-stabilization, this comparing and interfering aspect of the mind does not emerge. It is not just a one-time experience. It is about permanently and constantly abiding in the experience of pure consciousness. One lives with the firm conviction of one's true nature beyond the body and mind.

Self-realization without understanding is futile. Proclaiming that you have attained Self-realization based on a one-time experience is far from the truth. This is because the credit-taking mind is still present. One has not stabilized in that state.

Self-stabilization is the ultimate purpose of human life. If the body continues to indulge in old tendencies and habitual patterns even after many glimpses of Self-realization, then the glimpses have not served the ultimate purpose.

The judgmental mind surfaces again and again with imaginations and doubts about the experience of the Self. Due to the interference of the judging mind, the state of inner stillness remains veiled.

(29) *The importance of a living guru is that he ensures that you progress from Self-realization to Self-stabilization. A true guru teaches you to train the mind by instilling it with faith and understanding of the Truth so that the Self can experience itself without interference.*

Surrender of the judgmental mind is a prerequisite for Self-stabilization. With Self-stabilization comes Self-expression—the expression of the Self through the body–mind mechanism to fulfil the Self's potential. On attaining Self-stabilization at the age of thirty-five, the Buddha continued to spread the message of Truth till the ripe age of eighty. Siddhartha Gautama's body served as a medium for the Buddha state, the Self, to express itself.

(30) *When the purpose of Self-stabilization is not clear, you might mistake glimpses on the path as Self-realization and assume that to be the ultimate goal. If Self-realization is seen as Self-stabilization, then that is the ultimate goal. If you see it as a one-time experience, then it is just the beginning.*

Seeker 2: Thanks for clarifying the difference between glimpses and stabilization. I now understand that enlightenment should not be confused with one-off experiences. But what happens after Self-stabilization? How does it change our outlook?

Sirshree: Self-stabilization is the liberation from ego, from mechanical living, from all forms of bondage and preconceived notions. It is freedom from all defilements of the mind, such as fear, anger, hatred, greed, attachment, envy. Self-stabilization leads to abidance in the state of unbroken bliss, indescribable bliss that constantly asserts its eternal presence and pervades every aspect of life.

Everything in nature develops to its fullest potential. For instance, a flower blooms completely and fills the surrounding atmosphere with its fragrance. Similarly, every human being has infinite potential that can be expressed to the fullest. However, owing to ignorance, he remains entwined in false notions and creates roadblocks to his own progress.

As a result, he keeps away from the natural possibility of complete self-development. *When the Truth is understood not only intellectually but also at the experiential level, when all questions and doubts dissolve, that is the state of Self-stabilization. It entails the journey from the limited confines of the mind in the head to the unlimited expanse of the Self in the heart.*

After Self-stabilization, what happens is not change, but transformation. Change is just an alteration; transformation is a paradigm shift. For example, when you begin to climb the stairs to reach the terrace, you move from the first step to the second. Though this is a change, you are still on the stairs. When you move from the second step to the third, you can probably get a better view of the terrace, but you continue to be on the stairs. This is 'change'. When you move beyond the stairs onto the terrace, this is called a shift or 'transformation'.

With change, ignorance continues, because you still perceive from the level of the mind through judgments, logical premise, assumptions and memory. However, with transformation, the entire structure of the programmed mind is transcended. You rise above the stairs of mental perceptions and intuitively know from the terrace of the Self.

Suppose you are sitting in a room where there are pillars that block your view of the entire room. You keep changing your position in the room, so as to get a better view. However, you still cannot see the room in its entirety as the pillars obstruct a complete one-time view. But when you get into a helicopter that hovers above the room, you get a complete simultaneous view of everything as it is. You are also able to see what the others in the room are not able to see and which pillars are blocking their view.

In the same way, before Self-stabilization, you keep refining your perspective by going around the pillars of beliefs that block the experience of reality. You keep changing your perspective. However, rising beyond all beliefs, the mind is transcended; an all-encompassing reality is intuitively known by the Self. This is transformation.

After Self-stabilization, one transcends the opposites of happiness and sorrow, attachment and aversion, praise and censure, life and death. For example, it is a common belief that the Self-realized one becomes mild or humble. 'Becoming humble' presupposes the existence of a separate individual who has 'become' humble. However, stabilizing in the Self leads to the transcendence from both—ego and humility. There is liberation, not only from sorrow, but also from happiness. It is liberation from duality. The separate individual who says 'I have attained Self-realization' no longer exists.

Seeker 1: There was a phase when I was feeling peaceful and serene. But nowadays, I feel restless and disturbed. How can I be free from this restlessness?

Sirshree: In the journey of stabilizing in the experience of Self, it is important to understand the role of the judgmental mind, about how it keeps coming back amidst glimpses of Self-experience. During this journey, even if the judgmental mind keeps coming back a thousand times, let it happen. Treat it like the coming and going of clouds that temporarily veil the ever-present sunlight.

Like the eternal sunlight, Self-experience is constant. It neither comes nor goes; it neither increases nor decreases. Your awareness of Self-experience may reduce or can rise. When you have no worries—when nothing in the external world has occurred to increase your thoughts and there are no concerns about the future—the experience of Self seems more prominent. But when difficult situations arise, it seems as if the experience of Self is lost.

This can be understood, with the example of a TV that is switched on. The TV screen is lit up. However, in the afternoon, if the windows of the room are open to sunlight, then the TV screen will appear faint. Due to the brightness of sunlight in the room, you may not be able to clearly make out that the TV screen is lit-up. When windows are closed and curtains are drawn, then it may appear as if the TV screen has become brighter. But, you know that the TV screen is the same. It has neither dimmed, nor become brighter. It is just that you have become more aware of the screen that is always lit.

The judging and comparing nature of the human mind is just like a ball. It keeps bouncing back after a momentary glimpse of Self-experience. The mind can become frustrated and disappointed when it feels disconnected from the experience of Self. This happens due to the lack of understanding that these very feelings of frustration and disappointment are the cause and not the result of disconnectedness.

When you listen to the truth, you build conviction in the presence of the Self. Then again, like the ball, the judging and complaining mind bounces back, though not as much as it did earlier. In this way, the mind may bounce back numerous times, each time, quieting down a little, until a time comes when the mind becomes still and grounded. Allow the mind to rise; let go of the feelings of frustration and disappointment. You don't need to be worried every time it bounces back. Every time you watch the mind rising and falling, you develop conviction in your state of inner stillness that is constantly available behind the mind. With increasing conviction, the mind will gradually become still.

Seeker 1: What kind of thoughts arises after Self-stabilization?

Sirshree: Thoughts do not 'arise' in the mind after Self-stabilization. Rather, they are 'brought forth' voluntarily from the thoughtless state. Before Self-stabilization, thoughts occur at random. This is because man does not remember his real purpose.

Thoughts that arise after Self-stabilization are an expression only meant to help the attainment of the Truth through other bodies. This is because one has remembered the true Self and the purpose of this life on Earth. All those thoughts that used to arise when man was leading life believing that he was an individual body, come to an end.

On Self-stabilization, you are in the effortless state of pure being. Whether thoughts are there are not, does not affect you.

4

From Knowing to Not-knowing

Seeker 1: In my family, the Holy Scriptures are celebrated and recited during festivals. People take pride in reciting Sanskrit verses. I am not sure whether such recital can help. I wish to understand and practice the knowledge of the scriptures. Can the knowledge of the scriptures help me find the Truth?

Sirshree: You cannot borrow the Truth from outside; it cannot be obtained. This is because it is already available within you. When a true master points at the truth within you, it is by this grace that true wisdom awakens within you.

Truth is subjective experience, not objective knowledge. It cannot be known as you would the other topics of the world. You can only experience it by 'being' it. And to 'be' it, you need to empty yourself of all that you have learned about the Truth. You need to release all the beliefs that you have gathered this far. This requires true faith and devotion, which can be awakened in the presence of a living Guru.

The scriptures have been venerated as the Truth. They speak about the Truth; they can point to the Truth. The Truth expressed in the scriptures arose from the experience of the Self that realized masters revelled in. They are a reflection of the direct experience of the Truth. They serve as a mirror. But the mirror is not the Truth.

Moreover, the mirror is tainted with dust. The reflection of the Truth has been distorted through years of interpretation and commentaries, mostly by those who lacked the direct experience of the Self.

Consider the grand aphorism declared in the Upanishads – "Aham Brahmasmi". This declaration arose from the experience of the Self. This has been literally translated by many as "I am God", "I am that all-pervading reality". However, such translations cause the seeker to believe that he is the God personified. A person can never be God. The deeper import of the aphorism can be stated as, "God is the I-AM". This may sound grammatically incorrect. And yet, it means that God is the "I-AMness", the sense of existence, the living presence within every body-mind. This is what Jesus states as, "I AM that I AM". Interpretations and translations that do not arise from the experience of the Self mislead the seeker away from the essence of the Truth.

Seeker 1: But the scriptures originated from Self-realized masters.

Sirshree: When scriptures are transcribed, they are the expression of a realized master. The master bestows grace through the medium of words. But when one holds onto scriptures and invests in mere words and their empirical meanings, then one gets lost in the pointers and loses what they are pointing at.

When you enjoy a candy, you eat the candy and throw away the stick on which it was held. Words are like the stick. They are meant to be conveying the essence, which is beyond words. Once the essence is grasped, the role of words is over.

Commentaries and interpretations of the Truth lack the potency of the realized master's presence. The teachings and the instructions delivered by the living Guru have a very deep impact. If you try to hit someone with a bullet held in your hand, the bullet won't have an impact. But the Guru is like a gun. When the bullet is shot from the gun it hits the person with tremendous momentum and has a grave impact on him. In the same way, if the disciple listens to the Truth from someone else, then the impact is like the bullet thrown from the hand. When the disciple listens to the same words, the same knowledge, from the living Guru, his ego is eliminated. This is because the words delivered by the living Guru are directly coming from the experience of the Self; they arise from the Source – the quintessence of Truth.

Seeker 2: What are the hurdles in proceeding with self-study and analysis of spiritual books or scriptures?

Sirshree: Suppose the eyeglasses were to say that they want to see the eyes, what would you tell them? You would tell them, "You cannot see. You are only a medium through which the eyes see the world." The glasses cannot see the eye. It is the eye that sees through the glasses. In the same way, the human body-mind can never know the Self. It is the Self that experiences and expresses itself through the human body-mind.

You can continue to stuff the mind with conceptual knowledge, ornate with logical reasoning, but all this has nothing to do with the true Self. The mind imagines the Self in terms of the concepts that have been imprinted in memory. Concepts create barriers. To be able to experience the immaculate Self, one needs to unlearn what one has held as knowledge.

It is only with true faith and devotion that one can let go of such bookish knowledge and abide in the Truth. It is then that true realization of the depth and grandeur of the Truth becomes evident. Else, one loses it in intellectual delights of knowledge that is available in poetic lines, scriptural verses and hearsay. Such knowledge does not serve the real purpose.

The ego needs to realize that it is a hurdle in the experience of the Truth. A person is searching for God in the temple and enquiring, "Where is God? I've searched him all around here. I can't find him." He will be told, "God is standing right behind you, but is hidden because you are standing tall. You only need to bend low and bow down, and He will be revealed."

The highest use of the intellect is in realizing its own limitations. The highest use of reasoning is in realizing the limited confines of logic when it comes to experiencing the Truth.

The intellect should be trained for subtler contemplation to a point where it realizes the futility of stuffing knowledge. True wisdom lies in becoming empty. Become an empty flute through which divine music can flow.

Seeker 2: You said that Truth exists beyond words. Is there no way at all that it can be expressed?

(37) **Sirshree:** *The whole world of forms and phenomena is the expression of the Truth, the Self. It can be said that all that exists is the Truth, the Self, God, Consciousness – whatever you like to call it. But the mind cannot grasp this. When you seek God in terms of what you already know, it poses a hurdle in experiencing what is so obvious.*

True Wisdom is experiential. True Wisdom can be called '*Knowlerience*'. This is a new word that is needed to explain this. Prevalent words like "knowledge" and "experience" instantly bring up preconceived notions that are held within you. A new vocabulary is required to transcend these notions and interpreted meanings.

'*Knowlerience*' is the realization of the Truth through non-conceptual experience. Non-conceptual, because, it cannot be grasped through concepts, it cannot be known through thinking, it cannot be deduced through reasoning.

The Self cannot be explained in words, but it can be pointed at. However, there is a risk that the seeker of Truth may get caught up with the pointers and completely miss what they are pointing at.

A young child once asked his father what the colour green looked like. The father, whose finger was stained with red ink, pointed the stained finger in the direction of a tree and said, "That's green." The child, instead of looking at the tree beyond the two of them, fixed his gaze on his father's stained finger and said, "Yes. I understand."

You can see that he has mistaken the red stain on his father's finger to be green. The child then carries this misunderstanding with him throughout his life after mistaking the colour of the pointing finger to be the colour of what was being pointed at.

In the same way, people may spend their lifetime imprisoned in the limitations of thoughts and yet, they may claim to have experienced the Self. But, like the young child in this example, they really do not truly know it through direct experience.

One may say, "I can feel the presence of the Self." Another may say, "The experience of the Self is blissful." and yet another may say, "The Self cannot be described." These statements have nothing to do with the real experience of the Self. These are mere qualifying statements that arise as thoughts – and thoughts can never define the Self. The most we can do is to point to the Self.

The Self has been pointed at in various ways. Many who have realized the Self have written, spoken, and sung about it. But all these forms of expression are merely pointers, nothing more than stained fingers!

Many seekers spend their lives paying attention to the pointers instead of to what they are pointing. They argue about them all through their lives; they never look beyond these pointers.

Pointers belong in the realm of thoughts. The Self is from where thoughts originate. Thinking about the experience of the Self has nothing to do with actually experiencing the Self. When you look past these pointers and experience consciousness, you experience freedom from the shackles of concepts.

Seeker 2: This seems paradoxical. Whatever comes from you too is nothing but thoughts, expressed as words. As you said, they are not the essential wisdom. But somehow, your words seem to have a quieting effect on me. I feel peaceful and at ease.

Sirshree: With anything that you absorb from the world, you fill your mind. You stuff yourself with input that does not serve the real purpose. For example, whatever you hear on the TV or the radio, be it entertainment or information from the Discovery channel will fill you up. They will unconsciously cause impressions in your subconscious mind. You become fixated with these impressions.

Words arising from Truth serve you by emptying your mind. They bring about an un-conditioning of the mind. They break your attachment to the body-mind, so that you can see everything as-it-is.

The words that arise from Truth are like the fire-stick, which is used to push all other twig-sticks into the fire. Finally, when all the sticks have burnt, the fire-stick is also cast into the fire. In the same way, the words of Truth help in eradicating all false beliefs and preconceived notions in the fire of wisdom. At the end, when the mind becomes pure, then the words of Truth also dissolve. All that remains is the inexpressible experience of the Self.

However, when intellectual people are told this, they cast away the fire-stick well before all the other sticks are burnt. They say, "If I have to throw this fire-stick anyways, then why not now…" Such people need to be told that they should hold onto the fire-stick till the very end. Otherwise, they may wander away from the Truth. You have to hold onto the words of Truth because they help in emptying you of all concepts, until such time that you are established in Self-experience.

How do you know whether words are arising from the Truth? It is by the sense of tranquillity that you experience. You move away from the head, which is boiling with thoughts, and enter the heart, where there is pure silence, pure being.

Seeker 1: How do we attain that state beyond knowledge?

Sirshree: The question to be asked is – who is aspiring to attain that state beyond knowledge? Who is trying to grasp the experience of Self? Is the mind going to experience it? No.

The mind desires to be present and know the experience of the Self. It is only when the judging and aspiring mind drops, that the Self can experience itself. You need to reach the state of trans-ignorance. *Trans-ignorance is not the ignorance of the mind. It is the openness of the mind to whatever is. The mind no longer holds fixations or makes stories out of what is being experienced. One transcends both knowledge and ignorance and begins to experience life just like a child. One rests in the peace of 'not knowing' and allows life to unfold in a state of wonder.*

When you stop labelling what is being experienced in terms of whatever is already known, every experience becomes fresh, as if it's the first time. The world, that was appearing dead and dull due to the curtain of labels, begins to appear lively and vibrant. The light of beingness shines in everything that is being known.

This light of beingness cannot be found in books. It can only be experienced within yourself in pure silence, beyond noise and quietude, beyond thoughts, beyond everything that is known. It is the light of knowing, of awareness in which you perceive not only light, but also darkness.

When people do not recognize this light of knowing, which is constantly illumining their lives, they tend to be lost in whatever is being known. Spiritual knowledge and religious doctrines are food for the intellect, they belong to the world that is being known; they have nothing to do with the experience of the ultimate knower.

The entire knowable universe exists within the perspective of the human camera. The ultimate knower exists outside this camera. Outside the camera lies the domain of only One, of oneness. And when there is only One, it cannot be even called 'one', for there is neither one nor many. It can be called as the experience of 'nothing-everything' in so much as words can convey.

Seeker 2: Right. I have read about the Truth being the experience of nothingness. But there are others who argue that Truth is experienced by embracing totality – that it is everythingness.

Sirshree: With the Truth, there can be no two, no many. Debates and contradictions imply duality and happen when the One Truth is lost. Debates need to have two opposing ideologies or beliefs. And ideologies and beliefs have nothing to do with the Truth.

There are many who debate about the forms of God. There are others who debate whether God is formless or has a form. There are worshippers of Lord Shiva, who are in disagreement with the worshippers of Lord Vishnu. There are people who do not believe in form, who are at war with those who believe in a God that has form. Both are unable to see the One Truth.

Both these factions are actually watching the same movie. The first half of the movie depicts a God that has form and the latter half depicts a formless God. *Form is an essential means to realize the formless. The Formless cannot be known without a Form. And a*

Form cannot exist without the formless. With the direct experience of the Self, the duality of form and formlessness is resolved into the One reality that encompasses both.

The experience of the Self is that of Nothing with the potential of Everything. It is not the no-thing that the mind imagines as the absence of everything. It is Nothing that encompasses everything. It is the source of all possibilities. It is the creator of the manifest universe.

Seeker 2: Thank you for this clarity. It is so true that differences in these ideologies have caused a divide between religions of the world. People wage wars in the name of religion.

Sirshree: When people fight in the name of religion, their premise has nothing to do with the Truth, which is rooted in absolute Oneness. All originators of the prevalent religions were realized souls, be it the masters through whom Upanishads were expressed, or Jesus, or the Buddha, or Mahavira, or Prophet Mohammed, or Guru Nanak. They all expressed the Light of Consciousness and the Love for Oneness.

Consider that Jesus was never a Christian. Christian faith developed after Jesus. Buddha was never a Buddhist. Buddhist faith developed after the Buddha. Differences among the Christian, Muslim or Buddhist followers have been brought about by religion-mongers, who could not grasp the essence of their teachings. They have misused religion to propagate their individual faiths and create divides by perpetrating hatred and antagonistic beliefs.

Seeker 1: So how does the experience of the Self come about?

Sirshree: You allow the experience of the Self by immersing yourself in the love of the Self, by surrendering yourself to divine will. It is only when the individual personality vanishes through understanding that the Self reveals itself to itself.

Return to the innocence of a child, where you live in the wonder of 'not-knowing' and allow life to unfold. With this alone can you break free from the prison, bound by beliefs and philosophies.

The Truth is an open secret; it is so obvious that one easily misses it. Suppose you are searching for a bar of chocolate in a house. You search everywhere, in the drawing room, in the kitchen, in the bedrooms; you search every nook-and-corner; you go through each and every drawer and closet, but are unable to find it. How would you feel like if you were then told that the entire house, its walls, furniture, everything… is made of chocolate!

All the time, you were in frenzy, searching the chocolate in a particular wrapper… and so, you were missing what was obvious all the time. In the same way, the Truth is enlivening every aspect of your life. *The presence of the Self is the underlying essence of every moment that you are alive. Yet, you miss it, because you seek it in the wrappers of concepts and ideologies.*

Who-you-truly-are is already free. The notion of bondage is a myth. Freedom from this myth is true liberation. For this, nothing needs to change outside. The mind needs to be open, receptive, and non-assuming. There is one sentence that you can remember and repeat in every life situation: "All I know is that I don't know". Be open and receive life as it unfolds.

5

Transcending the Mind

Seeker 1: Why is it that the experience of the Self – which as you say, is the most obvious – is missed? If that can be pointed at, it may perhaps help me.

Sirshree: The primary hurdle in the experience of the Self is the assumed individual identity, which you refer to as 'I'. When an individual identity is assumed, it gives birth to the illusion of a separate 'I', confined within the boundaries of your body. With the birth of this illusory separate 'I', whatever happens with your body-mind, seems to happen to a 'me', whatever belongs at the body-level becomes 'mine'.

Whatever is inside the skin is considered as 'me' and everything else outside is assumed to be 'not me'. We have been living this myth without questioning it, because we find everyone else around us living with the same illusion.

This illusion is complete when the flip side of "I... me... mine" is also *imagined* into existence. Whatever is 'not me' is perceived as 'you… we… they… it'. This illusion is the root cause of all suffering, struggle and various defilements such as fear, anger, hatred, ill will, and jealousy. It shrouds the experience of who-you-truly-are.

Forgetfulness of who-you-truly-are leads to false identification with who you are not. You've become so addicted to the beliefs and stories that constitute the false personality that you continually try to improve and better this personality. But you are not this personality. It appears to be so due to the illusion of the mind.

The mind is a bundle of thoughts in which each thought is linked to a point of reference – the 'I'. This point of reference called 'I' is a false notion that keeps changing every moment.

If you carefully observe how you use the 'I' in your daily life, you will realize its fallacy. Consider the following sentences that one commonly speaks.

My hand was wounded when I had been to the workshop.

I was scared when I found that my hand was bleeding profusely.

I then thought of visiting the doctor to dress up the wound.

When one says, "I had been to the workshop", the word 'I' is being used to refer to the body. You keep saying many such things during the day by assuming yourself as the body. I had food, I climbed the stairs, I laughed etc. Here 'I' refers to the body.

The same sentence also says, 'My hand was wounded'. Whom does the 'My' refer to? If the earlier identification with the body were to be used, one would have said, "I was wounded." When you say, 'My hand was wounded', you consider yourself the owner of your body. It is only when you assume yourself to be separate from the body that you can say 'My hand'. Thus, you can see that the point of reference for the 'I' has shifted from the body to the owner of the body.

When you say, "I was scared", the 'I' in this context refers to the mind. The body cannot feel scared. The mind feels scared just as it also feels sad or elated, moody or ecstatic.

"I thought of visiting the doctor." Here again, the reference has shifted from the mind to the intellect. Thinking is considered an intellectual faculty. Here you assume yourself to be the intellect.

From this example, you can understand how the point of reference is false and also how it keeps changing. The use of the words 'I', 'Me', 'Mine' differs in various contexts. This was an example of only three sentences.

Upon deeper reflection, you will come across innumerable identities of 'I'. Different identities of 'I' spring into awareness at different points in time. However, due to delusion, you always believe it to be the same 'I'. Being lost in this delusion, the real 'I' remains in the dark. Your true nature never gets an opportunity to shine forth as it is eclipsed by these false identities.

So long as you are entrapped in these false identities, the experience of the Self remains shrouded.

Seeker 2: Spiritual disciplines prescribe ways of cleansing the mind off defilements like anger, greed, fear, and guilt, so that the mind can comprehend the Self. These deal with controlling these feelings and eradicating them by choosing virtues.

Sirshree: Negative emotions like anger or fear are played out through the body impulsively as a result of prior conditioning of the subconscious mind due to lack of awareness.

These emotions are symptoms of the root cause, which is identification with an idea of a separate individual 'I'. Egotism, anger or arrogance forms the secondary or false ego. People spend their lifetime trying to control the false ego. But that's of no use as long as the root cause is not addressed.

When you enquire into the nature of who-you-truly-are by investigating the 'I' who is getting angry or sad, you are stripping off the layers of false identity, which enmesh you. When this investigation is practiced relentlessly, who-you-truly-are is automatically revealed. When you honestly contemplate on who you 'are not', what remains at the end is who-you-truly-are – the Self, pure consciousness.

This is why enquiring into the nature of the body-mind, who you are not, is the direct way of being in the Self. You mentioned that the mind comprehends the Self. *Again, the mind can never comprehend the Self. When the unnecessary facet of the mind drops, the Self reveals itself to itself. There is nothing here for the mind. The mind does not stand to gain anything. Self-realization happens when the mind is prepared to lose itself in the love of the Self.*

Seeker 1: When the mind loses itself then how can we function in our life? The mind is the epitome of human evolution. It has led to human advancement. It helps us in daily functioning. How can we drop the mind?

Sirshree: You don't need to drop the mind in its entirety. No. You're not being told to stop thinking. Understand this carefully.

Our mind is originally like pure water, which clearly reflects the presence of the Self. However, it becomes impure when impregnated with thoughts of the individual 'I'. It is these thoughts that are the grime of ego. The intake of impure water is harmful to health. Just as pure water is vital for the health of the body, similarly it is essential to have a pure mind that reflects the presence of the Self.

All of us have an aspect of mind that can be called the Contrast mind. During infancy, every child abides in the experience of the Self. However, as the child grows, the parental programming and social conditioning lead to the formation of the contrast mind.

The contrast mind is that facet of the mind that discriminates, compares and judges everything. It is the constant chatter that ceaselessly comments about everything that is experienced. Just like the contrast control on a TV remote, which is denoted by a circle with black and white halves, the contrast mind too dwells in duality.

The contrast mind divides everything into silos and labels objects, beings, or circumstances as good or bad, happy or sad, black or white, dark or light, positive or negative, low or high, benefit or loss, and so on. It dwells in fixations of duality. It draws assumptions about everything. Whenever we notice ourselves thinking: "This shouldn't have happened… That should have happened… Why does it always have to be me? Life is so difficult… When will these people change", it is this contrasting aspect of the mind that is at work.

The other facet of the mind is the intuitive mind, which functions spontaneously based on natural intuition and inspiration. Unlike the contrast mind, the intuitive mind is focused on the present task and performs it to the best of its ability. It is free from comparison, judgment, labelling and fixation. Thoughts of the intuitive mind are harmless and constructive.

An example can help understand these facets of the mind. When you are scurrying down the stairs, it is the intuitive mind that is functioning. It happens spontaneously and rhythmically. However, while going down the stairs, if you get a thought, "I am climbing down the stairs so well… Uh oh… I only hope I don't trip and fall", this is the contrast mind in action.

Invariably, when the contrast mind intervenes, you may have found that you tend to either miss or jump a step, disturbing the rhythm in which you were climbing down the stairs.

The contrast mind causes us to be stuck in the vicious cycle of polarities such as pain and pleasure, praise and blame, success and failure, fame and shame, joy and sorrow, love and hatred. This facet of the mind is caught up in imagined notions, presumptions and beliefs. This triggers fear, worry, anger and depression. It is this facet of the mind that dwells in past memories or the anxieties of the future. Due to this, the present moment is lost to us.

These characteristics of the contrast mind do not allow us to accept the present moment as it is. Non-acceptance of the present moment is the root cause of all sorrow and disease. It is this contrasting nature of the mind that causes disease and depression. It is due to the judging and vacillating nature of the contrast mind that people suffer from insomnia.

The contrast mind veils the experience of the Self. It is like the eclipse that hides the ever-present sun of consciousness. It is a facet of the mind that causes sorrow and disease. Hence it needs to be transcended to restore true happiness, peace and higher consciousness.

(51) *Being in the experience of the Self does not mean that you should be in a thoughtless state. Thoughts of the intuitive mind will continue to occur and enact through the body. For the experience of the Self, thoughts of the contrast mind need to be transcended.*

All activities will continue to happen in the best way. In fact, you will become more productive. When the contrast mind surrenders to the will of the Self, you will be able to use the skills of your body-mind more effectively by being in a peaceful happy state.

Seeker 1: How does the contrast mind shroud the Self? What is its malfunction that prevents the experience of the Self?

Sirshree: The contrast mind poses major roadblocks in being in the experience of pure consciousness. There are various patterns of the contrast mind that you need to be consciously aware of when they are being played out.

(52) *Holding expectations regarding Self-realization is a major impediment. The contrast mind tries to make a tangible goal out of everything that is pursued. However, being in the experience of the Self is not a tangible goal. Rather, the Self is the enlivening presence in which all pursuits of life are undertaken. Hence, positing a goal and defining expectations cannot lead to the experience of the Self.*

Since every external pursuit in life is quantified or qualified in material or tangible terms, the contrast mind tries to set expectations for the purpose of experiencing the Self as well. It will desire to experience such objectives as peace of mind, tranquillity, deeper intuition, or greater creativity. If it doesn't immediately see such results, it feels disappointed. It then gives up by assuming that the pursuit is impossible or futile.

The key is to see through all such expectations as the play of the contrast mind. *Being the Self is both, the means and the end in itself. You are already at the destination during the journey. You just need to be present and allow any such thoughts of expectations to pass by. Let feelings of disappointment or frustration arise and pass by, for they too are food for the contrast mind.*

Seeker 2: But then if there is nothing in particular to be pursued, wouldn't we feel lost with such seeking? Wouldn't it lead to boredom?

Sirshree: You cannot let go of expectations without completely understanding the truth. Doing so can lead to dullness and lack of purpose.

The contrast mind has no role to play in the experience of the Self. This may cause feelings of boredom. When the current state of mind is non-palatable and unexciting, the mind seeks avenues for excitement and indulges.

For instance, if you are seated in meditation, a few minutes might feel like you've been sitting for an hour. If the contrast mind resists this, the meditation may seem difficult to practice and you might even consider giving up.

It's important not to give up at such moments. Continuing to practice being in the stillness of conscious presence despite uncomfortable feelings brings its reward. *We shouldn't resist feelings of boredom but rather accept them as a part of the practice. We should continue to witness such feelings in a detached manner. As we persist, such feelings of boredom will pass away, revealing the experience of stillness.*

The other key pattern of the contrast mind is fixations. Many a times, we may feel we have had a particularly pleasant or unusual spiritual experience. The contrast mind then holds onto this past impression and expects to experience an identical experience again. In doing so, it jumps to conclusions and tries to predetermine the experience of the Self. It constantly compares the present experience with past impressions and causes dissatisfaction. It tries to fix the end result.

We should not be fixated about any one thing. Allow whatever is happening to happen, and let whatever is not happening not happen. We should be intent on experiencing the knower of these fixations. The ultimate purpose is not to know any particular experience we may have, but rather to experience the knower of these experiences.

Yet another hurdle in Self-experience is the blending of the sense of the body and the sense of presence of the Self.

The sense of the body serves as a pretext to experience the sense of Being. Body sensations – whether painful, pleasurable or neutral – serve as a medium to realize pure beingness, which is beyond the body.

However, the sense of the body is not the sense of conscious presence of the Self. The sense of the body and the sense of conscious presence co-exist and are blended together. This can cause confusion when the mind tries to seek the experience of the Self.

Seeker 2: How does this confusion come about?

Sirshree: Understand this with the help of an analogy. Two songs are being played simultaneously. One is being played softly in a low volume, while the other is loud and jarring. We are asked to listen to the soft song and not confuse the two together. Initially, we may find it difficult, because the loud song draws our attention. However, when we train ourselves to attend to the soft song and recognize it when it is being played in isolation, then we begin to successfully spot it even amidst loud noise.

Meditation is the practice of silencing the loud noise of thoughts, to gain recognition of the soft song of Beingness that is constantly present in the background. When one clearly recognizes one's Being, one can then experience it even in the din and roar of the marketplace.

The contrast mind tries to seek the experience of the Self in body sensations, thoughts and feelings. It conceptualizes and imagines the Self in terms of visuals, sounds, and sensations. This is a major hurdle in being in the stillness of the Self.

Many seekers assume that the Self can be experienced only in the absence of body sensations. They equate the body-less state with the sense of conscious presence. Loss of body sensations has nothing to do with the experience of the Self. We can rest in the sense of presence of the Self despite painful or pleasurable sensations in the body.

Meditation on the Self helps in building conviction in the song of presence of consciousness that is being played constantly in the background of thoughts, feelings and body sensations. When you develop clear recognition of this presence, then you cannot miss it. You cannot be lost to it thereafter. Does this answer your question?

Seeker 2: Yes it does. Thank you!

Sirshree: Yet another major hurdle of the contrast mind is its tendency to keep checking for the experience of the Self. The contrast mind can masquerade as a checker and attempt to judge the experience.

The contrast mind may try to assess the experience and pose doubts and questions such as, "Let me see who is experiencing this. Is this experience the same as the actual experience of the Self? Nothing special seems to be happening. Why am I not becoming thoughtless even after sitting for so long?"

Checking, comparing, and judging divert our focus from the experience of the Self. If we get entangled in this, the awareness of consciousness is lost. Whenever the contrast mind intervenes and tries to check the experience, know that it is a trap.

The judging and questioning mind cannot exist without the presence of the Self. The very fact that the contrast mind is functioning is indirectly indicating the presence of the Self. Whenever a checker thought arises, simply smile and observe it.

Know that the mind is playing a trick. We don't have to question our awareness; we only need to be present in awareness.

Taking credit for the experience of the Self is another major hurdle. With the experience of presence, the contrast mind takes credit for having experienced it.

Understand this with the example of an expert pianist who is rendering a symphony on the piano. When the performance reaches its peak, the pianist is lost in the performance. He does not exist at that time. All that exists is the performance. However, after the performance, the contrast mind enters and says, "I performed so well!"

By taking credit for experiencing the Self, the contrast mind self-appoints itself to the job of experiencing the Self. The Self experiences itself only when the contrast mind surrenders. Such surrender is not a blind surrender; it happens with the conviction that the experience of the Self is beyond the realm of the mind.

Whenever the contrast mind tries to take credit, we should realize that it is yet another trick. Tell the mind, "You cannot own the experience. It is only when you become still that the experience of the Self is revealed. To the extent that you are still, the experience will shine forth. The more you chatter, the greater the delay in the experience of the Self."

Seeker 1: How can these tricks of the contrast mind be put to rest?

Sirshree: You don't need to try doing something about it. These patterns of the contrast mind are played out in the dark, when you are not aware that it is happening. When you bring detached awareness into the play of the contrast mind, it leads to clarity and recognition.

Detached witnessing enables you to distance yourself from the mind and its works. When you are attached with the mind, you lend it energy. When you witness it detachedly, it loses its power to influence you. The patterns of the contrast mind begin to lose their power. However, the intuitive mind continues to function at its best.

The key here is to not resist the mind. Accept and allow the patterns and whims of the mind to surface. Watch them as they rise and fall. This, in itself, lays the contrast mind to rest. The mind begins to turn inward and get attuned to conscious awareness.

The mind begins to lose its conditioning. It begins to love and accept the truth of what is, as it is. Such a mind begins to abide in the present, without vacillating in the past or future. This makes it conducive for Self-illumination. The pure mind serves as a mirror for the Self to experience itself and express its divine qualities.

6

Discerning the Real Amidst the Unreal

Seeker: What is true wisdom? And what is the hallmark of true wisdom?

Sirshree: Wisdom is reflected through your presence. How are you present in the various situations of daily life? Where is your attention? Is it fixed on the permanent changeless reality – the very essence of life, or is it divested in the fleeting, changing aspects of the illusory world.

(62) *The essence of wisdom is Viveka - the power to discern the real amidst the unreal. It is the ability to discriminate between the Truth and illusion. It develops when you gain understanding of your true nature.*

(63) *Everything... everything that is being known is temporary, short-lived, it comes and goes. It is the ultimate knower alone, who is permanent, eternal and unshakable. The objective world has a beginning and end. Your body and your mind – which comprises*

thoughts and feelings – have a beginning and end. However, that which enlivens all this, that which is the knowing presence, is beginningless, birthless, endless.

The Self is beyond both subject and object. It is pure consciousness, in the presence of which both subject and object come into being. People keep asking what came first – the subject or the object, the chicken or the egg. Both arise together from the state of Self-at-rest.

The purpose behind creating this objective world of forms and phenomena does not lie in the details of the world. The whole and sole purpose is for the Self to experience itself through all these experiences.

64. *The experiencer experiences the experiencer in and through every experience.*

Being established in this experiential understanding is Self-stabilization. One gets established in the wisdom – Whatever is happening is with the body-mind… not with me… not to me… but for me. The whole and sole purpose of everything is that the Self experiences itself in and through the myriad experiences of the world through the body-mind.

65. *Shift your attention from the body-mind to ultimate experiencer – the Self. Turn back your attention from the objects of perception to that which enables perception, from thought to that which enables thinking. You will then rise above the changing and limited to that which is changeless, eternal and boundless.*

This understanding is both the path and the destination of spiritual seeking. *Whenever you go through any situation, be it a challenging work situation, or a testing time at home, a painful*

66.

experience at the body-level, remind yourself – It is not happening with you. It is not happening to who-you-truly-are. It is happening with the body.

Seeker: But there are tough situations when we feel disturbed by emotions.

Sirshree: Suppose you are cutting a thick cloth with scissors, and you hear the scissors complaining, "This cloth is so thick... It's so difficult to cut... Why has such a difficult cloth been given to me?"

In this case, you can clearly understand that these are the feelings of the scissors, the tool you are using. It is not your feeling. In the same way, you can observe feelings, thoughts and sensations arising in your body from the perspective of a detached witness. When you believe that you are this body-mind, when you assume that you are the tool that you are using, you get affected.

But as a detached witness you can tell yourself, "All this is not with me – the real 'I'. They keep coming and going in this wondrous tool that I use, my body–mind mechanism. The real "I", or consciousness, is the knower of this mechanism. I can witness everything that happens with the body-mind and know that they are temporary."

Seeker: Does that mean that with this understanding, there would be no pain?

Sirshree: Being a detached witness does not mean that there won't be pain. Body sensations will be felt. There can be pain at the body-level. However, there won't be sorrow due to the pain. The sorrow comes because of your attachment with the mind. When you are a detached witness you do not identify with the mind.

What is the mind? It is a bundle of thoughts. So any sorrow is nothing but resistance to what is happening. This resistance may cause emotions that are felt at the body-level. But again, these emotions, these sensations are not who-you-are. You are untouched – the ultimate knower of everything, the supreme living presence in which all this is being enacted.

True wisdom roots you in changeless presence. It establishes you in pure consciousness. Everything that appears is unreal. Thoughts, feelings, words, sensations, concepts, and objects are like clouds that come and go in the changeless sky of pure consciousness. To be able to discern the temporary nature of these and rest in awareness of pure consciousness is true wisdom.

Remembering this truth through every circumstance – not just painful, but also pleasurable, not just in suffering, but also when in joy – is true wisdom.

Seeker: Why do we tend to be entangled in the illusory façade of the world?

Sirshree: When we move through the ocean of worldly life, we tend to be enamoured by it to such an extent that we become oblivious of the transitory short-lived nature of the world.

How we experience the world has been programmed since childhood through our genes and particular upbringing. We function through this programming and fall a victim to our own likes and dislikes. We have made prisons for ourselves from the concepts and beliefs that we have borrowed through our upbringing.

We encounter situations in our daily lives where we are gripped by attachment to what we like and aversion to what we dislike. *Attachment and aversion are two sides of the same coin. They draw us away from our true nature that is rooted in changeless permanence. We either chase after seemingly pleasant experiences or avoid seemingly unpleasant experiences.*

Take the example of smoking. You may be allergic to smoking while your neighbour may relish it. Smoking being the same, why does it appear unpleasant to you when it is pleasant for your neighbour?

The nature of the world is neither pleasant nor unpleasant. It is what it is – without labels, without bias. It is how you relate to it from your past conditioning that makes the world appear in particular ways.

To add to this, you ascribe labels to the world – be it people or objects, situations or experiences. The moment you cover something up mentally with a label, you stop seeing the truth of it. Its essence is lost to you.

Your world is a screen upon which you project your own mental traits, your unresolved emotions, your strengths and deficiencies. What you view as the world is, in reality, a reflection of what you project.

Seeker: It's an intriguing fact… but I often wonder why different people react to the same events in vastly different ways?

Sirshree: *Incidents have no meaning by themselves, unless meanings* *are superimposed through thoughts. And the same incident can cause entirely different thoughts in different people.*

This is because they're projecting or superimposing their own mental baggage on the screen, then watching the scene through their own mental filters. When they do this, it distorts the picture of reality.

(72) *There is no absolute world out there. Rather, you are constantly shaping your own personalized world as you go through life. People, situations – everything you experience – are shaded by your perception and are projections of what is held deep within your mind.*

You mentally mould the personalities of people around you through your own beliefs and assumptions. Though it may seem unbelievable, you're actually attracting situations and people into your daily life according to the emotions, behavioural traits, strengths and deficiencies you harbour within your mind. You are lost in external details to such an extent that you don't realize these details are only living pictures of what lies buried within your mind.

(73) *External situations are not the cause, but rather a reflection of what you hold within. No incident or situation is a problem by itself. A situation is a situation as-is. It becomes a so-called problem or triggers blame or complaint within us only because we are viewing it through the filters of our limiting beliefs.*

The experiences that we go through in life are like mirages. What we see is not what actually is. We do not see things for what they truly are. If we have to see through the mirage, then we need to break through the very cause why the mirage appears to be so. The background that makes things appear frightening to you needs to be destroyed so that the truth behind the mirage can be seen clearly.

The judgmental and comparing faculty of the mind creates worrying and frightening apparitions. This faculty of the mind needs to be brought down.

Seeker: How can we avoid being entrapped by the conditioning of the mind? How can we comprehend the real amidst the unreal?

Sirshree: By learning the art of asking the right question to yourself in various life situations – questions that will lead you from what is obvious to the deeper transcendental truth. Such questioning can break through illusions that appear in various circumstances, so that you can smile when faced with any illusion, without getting deluded.

If you do not put up the right question before the mind, then it will verbalize the illusion in its own words and get entangled; it will complain and grumble, "Life is difficult; people do not cooperate; my children will abandon me; old-age is setting in"

How can you be in peace when plagued by such thoughts? *You need to learn the art of right questioning and apply it whenever you are caught up in such an illusive maze. Asking yourself the right question at the right time can remind you to shift your perspective from the obvious to the deeper truth.*

The question that can help you raise your awareness of the truth behind the mirage in daily situations is: "Is this a myth, a fact, a truth or the ultimate truth?"

As soon as you ask this question, your awareness will rise. You need to ask the right question to see through the assumptions, speculations and idiosyncrasies of the mind. As soon as you transcend the assumptions of the mind, you will begin to feel a natural state of peaceful stillness.

Seeker: How do we apply this question to break through the illusion?

Sirshree: Consider the example of wealth. If your thoughts are heavy, injured, insatiable and complaining, then even if you amass a lot of wealth, you will only buy a hell for yourself. Without an understanding of truth, even being wealthy becomes a curse. There are many rich people who are victims of stress, depression and disease. So money, by itself, is not the key to a happy life.

But there are people who keep complaining that their poverty is the main cause of their unhappiness. They need to ask, "Is this a myth? Aren't there people who are wealthier than me and yet unhappy?" The mind will gain clarity that it is indeed a myth. Asking this question gives a chance to break this myth.

The other part of the question is "Is it a fact?" And the answer is that it could be a fact, but then, "Is it the truth?" The truth about wealth is that every scene is a preparation for the next future scene. *You create your future by the seeds of feelings that you plant in the present. When you are gripped by feelings of despair and scarcity, you plant seeds of a future that you don't actually desire.*

However, when you have faith in this law, you will shift your feelings and honour abundance with faith. *The one who dwells in joy and faith, regardless of the situation-at-hand is truly wealthy! This uncompromising joy makes him a magnet that attracts the best things in his life.*

Is the water in this glass cold, or is it warm? The answer lies in relativity. If your left hand is cold, then the warm water may feel hot. If your right hand is hot, then the warm water may feel lukewarm. It then turns out that your left hand does not agree with the right hand on the temperature of the water. So your own body is lying to you. Both the hands are stating their facts, but none of them is telling the truth. The truth is that the water is neither hot nor cold.

The culminating part of this question is, "What is the ultimate truth… the bright truth… the absolute reality?" When you ask yourself this question, you are reminded of the ultimate truth that everything that is happening is only a medium for the Self to experience its nature and express its divine qualities. You shift from the limited personal standpoint to the universal standpoint of the Self.

Asking this question awakens you, it challenges your beliefs and throws light on the darkness that seems to engulf you.

The purpose of such questioning is to develop unshakeable clarity that you can be in bliss, regardless of innumerable ominous problems that seem to loom over you. It is to gain maturity that tides may continue to rise and fall, but you remain untouched, unsullied and carefree forever.

You need to inculcate this habit of asking the right questions – Why do I fear death? Why do I fear disease? What is it that I exactly fear? And why? Who am I assuming myself to be?

You need to ask the right question at the right time. People tend to ask the wrong questions, which lead them into further quandary. Or else, they tend to ask the right questions at the wrong time.

Seeker: Thank you… I will practice asking this question when situations tend to pull me down.

Sirshree: *Every decision you take, every choice you make, conveys whether you are trapped in the illusion of your mental world or in clarity and conviction of your true nature.*

Seeker: You mentioned about being a detached witness to whatever is happening with the body-mind. Is there any way I can tide through negative situations and remember the truth?

Sirshree: It is the thoughts that you entertain in the situations that shake you up. Thoughts that are impoverished, heavy and injured can cause you to see darkness in bright daylight.

If you've travelled by train, you would have experienced that it becomes dark when the train passes through a tunnel. What do you do when the train passes through the tunnel? Your attention suddenly turns within, as there is nothing to watch outside in the darkness. Your gaze is fixed on the other mouth of the tunnel, where bright daylight appears. You know that it's just a matter of time before you will be out of the darkness of the tunnel in the brightness of daylight.

In the same way, whenever situations that cause negative feelings like sorrow, disappointment, anger, or despair occur, remind yourself:

"I am joy that is travelling through this tunnel of sorrow"

"I am peace travelling through this tunnel of anger"

"I am bright faith, travelling through this tunnel of despair."

You will say so with the firm conviction that this negative feeling is merely a temporary occurrence in the eternity of love, bliss and peace. Your attention will be focused on the brightness of love, bliss, and peace that will shortly unfold when you are out of the tunnel of negativity.

For this, you need to be aware of the negative thoughts and feelings that arise from the contrast mind. Whenever such thoughts of complaints, suffering, fear, anger or hatred engulf you in circumstances, your awareness will remind you that these are temporary.

When you lack awareness, you forget the temporary nature of these thoughts and feelings and get entrapped in them. Being entrapped in them, you plant seeds of negativity, which attract even more negativity in your life. These seeds bind you and do not allow you to open up to the free flow that comes from the Self.

Verbalizing such affirmations helps in reminding yourself and raising your awareness to rise above the situation tunnel that you are going through.

7

The Path of Wisdom

Seeker 1: How do I progress towards enlightenment? There are various paths that are popular in the scriptures. Which path is more effective?

Sirshree: There are many paths that lead to stabilization in Self-experience, such as Gyana (Wisdom), Dhyana (Meditation), Karma (Action), Japa (Chanting), Self-Enquiry, Bhakti (Devotion), etc. But they can broadly be divided into just two – the Path of Wisdom and the Path of Devotion.

The Path of Devotion is that of surrender to the divine will of God. It is the path of submitting to Consciousness–the Source of everything. Effort in this path is effortless, as actions happen in joyous surrender to the Self.

The Path of Wisdom is that of will power, where the seeker of Truth applies his intellect to grasp the Truth and internalize it.

The Path of Devotion is akin to a kitten, which leaves its body loose and gives itself up to its mother, who then carries it around with her mouth. The Path of Wisdom is like that of a baby monkey that needs to clasp onto its mother's belly when she jumps from one branch to the other. The kitten surrenders. The baby monkey clutches with all its might.

All the paths that are known in spirituality finally culminate in this two-fold path – one approach is that of complete surrender, while the other is that of intellectual reasoning and meditation. The seeker of Self-realization needs guidance on both these paths.

Seeker 1: So do both these paths lead to the same result?

Sirshree: Understand this with the help of an example. There were two travellers who needed to cross safely through a jungle to return home. One of them was blind, while the other did not have legs. Individually, they could not have made it home. The lame traveller climbed on the shoulders of his blind companion and guided him through the jungle. The blind man followed his directions and walked carefully, carrying him through the jungle. Both managed to reach home safely.

So it is on the path of Self-realization. The lame man symbolizes the eye of wisdom, while the blind one represents the legs of devotion. Without the legs of devotion, the eyes of wisdom cannot walk the path. The legs of devotion cannot see the path without the eyes of wisdom. Let devotion obtain the eyes of wisdom and let wisdom in turn receive the legs of devotion.

The seeker who pursues the path of wisdom through the practice of meditation and conscious action develops unswerving faith, thereby leading to the surrender of his individual personhood to the Self. The one who follows the path of devotion matures in understanding of the Truth.

Finally the one who works for attaining wisdom surrenders, and the one who surrenders attains wisdom. Thus, both the paths merge at its culmination in Self-realization.

Tejgyan is that understanding that culminates these paths - those on the path of wisdom attain devotion and those on the path of devotion attain wisdom.

Seeker 1: So then, how do I start? Which path do I choose to start the journey?

Sirshree: With Tejgyan, you begin directly with the understanding that brings together both Wisdom and Devotion. You do not have to decide which path is best for you.

Whatever the mind prefers need not be the best path for you. Following the path that the mind feels like is like asking a thief how he would like to be captured. The thief would never give away the path that would lead to his downfall. Similarly, the aspect of the mind that considers itself as a separate individual has to drop. That aspect of the mind cannot be trusted to decide which path to tread. Leave how this happens to grace. Ultimately, grace is the only way.

Seeker 2: What is the crux of the path of wisdom?

Sirshree: The reference point from where you see the world is the crux of wisdom. When the mind is assumed to be the knower of the world, it distorts the view of reality. Without wisdom, one uses the mind as the reference point to look at life. The beliefs and notions held by the mind skew our view of the world. True wisdom is about transcending the individuality, the false personal sense of the being the body.

With Tejgyan, one begins to detach from the mind and comprehend every aspect of life from the standpoint of pure consciousness. True wisdom enables the seeker to start with the Self as the reference point. *When people seek the Truth, considering themselves as the body-mind, they can never arrive. With the right wisdom, one realizes that there is no need to arrive; one is already home, in one's true nature.*

The essence of this wisdom is to build conviction in the truth that you are not the body; you are not the mind; you are not anything that is being known; you are the absolute knower; you are the knowing essence. Who-you-truly-are is the experiencer experiencing itself in and through every experience. It is this understanding that makes wisdom complete.

The crux of wisdom is to realize and be established in the firm conviction that nothing is happening with you; nothing at all is happening to you. Everything – whether pleasurable or painful – is happening with the body-mind. It is this conviction that constitutes 100% Wisdom.

Seeker 1: How is the path of wisdom different from the path of karma or meditation?

Sirshree: Both, Karma-yoga –the path of right action – and Dhyana-yoga –the path of meditation – are actually practices

100% Wisdom

of wisdom. Wisdom or right understanding is the essence of meditation. Wisdom is also essential for conscious karma.

Conscious karma is wisdom-in-action. The seeker applies effort to transmute higher understanding into action. All activity that you undertake is only meant to serve the higher purpose of Self-realization and Self-expression.

The practice of conscious action backed by higher understanding naturally leads the seeker into the experience of the Self. When actions are performed with the recognition of the Self, every action serves as an opportunity, an invitation to honour the divine presence that enlivens it.

Meditation is the state of being absorbed in the Self. Meditation is your essential nature. Meditation, when viewed as a practice, is a way of stilling the mind. The practice of meditation helps you detach from thoughts that plague your awareness. It raises awareness of pure consciousness. Without the right wisdom of your true nature, practicing meditation is futile. Thus, wisdom is the precursor to both meditation and action.

Since both meditation and karma are aspects of the Path of Wisdom, both ways, finally culminate in devotion.

Seeker 3: This is wondrous! Thank you. This really helps to clarify the importance of right understanding. We can start anywhere and we'll naturally reach the same destination – the Self.

Sirshree: Yes. *Ultimately, the experience that karma, devotion, meditation and wisdom lead to is one and the same. Performing karma in the spirit of wisdom is true devotion. Performing awakened action*

in the light of recognition of the Self is devotion.

Seeker 1: Great! This statement encompasses all the so-called paths – karma, wisdom and devotion. Till today, I have been reading and believing them to be separate paths, but now I am beginning to see how these three are integrally one.

Sirshree: Mere intellectual understanding of this does not suffice. You know about the Truth; but you need to live it. This understanding should permeate all action. This is where devotion plays an important role.

(85) *There are many intellectually heavy seekers who believe that they can do with intellectually understanding the Truth. They believe that devotion is not their cup of tea. They need to realize that wisdom can function only through the medium of devotion.*

There are people who flaunt their knowledge and indulge in intellectual discussions. The only result is intellectual entertainment. It does not serve to drop their ego.

(86) *There is risk, inherent with acquiring knowledge. Knowledge is mere information. It can cause one to feel egotistic. When one believes that one knows, one shuts his ears to further learning.*

(87) *True wisdom is beyond knowledge. True wisdom comes with devotion, with the attitude of surrender to life. It comes with unconditional acceptance to the way life unfolds.*

There are also people who take pride in leading a *sattvic* way of life – a life of piety, equanimity and balance. They consider a sattvic way of life as their ultimate goal.

Seeker 2: Yes. I've read about the merits of being sattvic. It is also said that being in equanimity is true yoga.

Sirshree: Everyone would love to become sattvic after getting to know its virtues. Sattva provides composure, level-headedness, purity and virtuousness. Sattvic people are sensitive to the effects of food on the body and mind. They eat well-balanced and optimum amount of food. They make optimum use of sleep, activity and rest. They do not overindulge. They tread the middle path.

However, here's a word of caution. *Being sattvic is not the ultimate goal of life. There are dangers of remaining stuck with the sattvic way of life without seeking to go beyond it.*

Seeker 2: I was of the opinion that equanimity can help in stilling the mind and being in the experience of Self. How could being sattvic be dangerous?

Sirshree: *To be able to understand the state beyond Sattva, you need to first understand that Sattva is the temperament of your body, mind and intellect; it is not your quality.* You are not your body, mind or intellect. Your essential nature is consciousness, the Self. The Self presides over the body, mind and intellect. You are the master of your temperament.

Many people who take to spirituality consider the progression to a sattvic way of life as the final goal. There are dangers inherent in resting on the plateau of Sattva, without transcending it.

The state that is beyond sattva is known as the *Gunateet* state – the state that transcends the temperaments of your body-mind mechanism. It is the state of pure consciousness.

(90) *The biggest danger of remaining stuck with sattva is the probability of backsliding into lethargy. If sattvic people are unaware that there is something beyond sattva, they can become complacent, egoistic and arrogant.*

Seeker 2: But people of sattvic nature perform unselfish deeds for the good of others. Doesn't this contribute to their progress?

Sirshree: There is no harm in unselfish service, as long as they are truly selfless. People of sattvic nature tend to take credit for performing altruistic deeds for the wellbeing of society. True wisdom lies in surrendering all deeds to the Self. However, they revel in a sense of self-pride for being the doer of noble deeds.

(91) *Being bound by negative karma is like being bound to iron handcuffs. However, being attached to virtuous deeds is like being bound to golden handcuffs. Even if they are golden, they are handcuffs after all… they bind you.* One cannot easily discern this subtle form of bondage. While avoiding negativity is good, being attached to positive deeds can stall your progress. Sattva-predominant people need to progress by transcending both – negative and positive deeds.

(92) "I know it all" is a very dangerous belief. *People who have the arrogance of "I know it all" can get trapped in the mire of Sattva. They tend to be lost in intellectual delights and flaunt their knowledge of spirituality. Such knowledge is mere information, not true wisdom. True progress happens only when one becomes empty off all notions and abides like an empty flute, through which divine music can be played.*

It can be considered unfortunate for someone who has come near the ultimate state to then backslide due to complacency or arrogance.

Seeker 1: We see most people aspiring for a balanced life and limit themselves to virtuous actions. This is a revelation that merely being virtuous and balanced can also be risky.

Sirshree: It is risky if you consider it as the final goal. You've got to move further and transcend it.

Seeker 2: There are certain spiritual disciplines that state that we should awaken our Kundalini by opening our chakras to attain enlightenment. Is this path an alternative to wisdom?

Sirshree: If there is a desire to experience mystical sensations or bright light within, then it is like searching for the experience of the Self on the body. This is the biggest hurdle in Self-realization. *The mind likes to fantasize and seek the experience of the Self at the mental or physical level. The mind aspires to know and measure everything in its own terms. The experience of Self is the source of life. It cannot be measured or known by the mind's scale.*

All the experiences, which the mind comes across, are fleeting. They exist for a short period of time and then diminish. The mind then keeps yearning for the same experiences again and again. Out of ignorance, man may continue to repeatedly long for the same experiences at the body-mind level.

Very often, experiences that seem to be very gratifying and pleasurable to the mind are major hindrances. The sense of pure presence, of pure awareness, is the ultimate experience. You need not look for any other experience. Till now, you have believed that "I am bound", "I need to attain liberation". However, as your understanding deepens, you realize that you are already liberated. *Self-realization is your original nature, and it is always accessible to you. It is not dependent on the chakras of your energy-body.*

Many people believe that one can behold the brightness of a thousand suns after awakening of kundalini. Such beliefs complicate spirituality. *Awakening the kundalini is only related to the body; be clear that it has nothing to do with Self-realization. Self-experience is the simplest and most obvious experience, which is always going on. Its utter simplicity becomes a problem for the mind that likes to fantasize it.*

Even if your body experiences mystical sensations, or sees some divine light, it is very important to understand this: In which light did you see that light? *You need light to see anything. However, there is also the invisible light in which you can see light itself! This invisible light is that of awareness, the inner knowing. It is beyond the realm of sights, sounds and sensations.*

When that light is witnessed, awareness becomes aware of itself. The light of consciousness, which shines upon everything becomes self-illumined. The Self experiences its own presence.

You do not have to get stuck at these experiences of light or sound because the true experience of the Self lies in experiencing consciousness, which enables the seeing of light or darkness.

A living Guru knows such risks that can entrap the seeker. He prods the seeker to move further so that the seeker transcends the realm of body and mind and gets established in the Self.

Seeker 1: Is a Guru essential in the spiritual journey?

Sirshree: Is a Guru required? The answer to this is simple: Is a mother required? The answer to both the questions is the same. There are some children who don't have mothers and yet they grow and thrive. There are a few who didn't have a Guru and yet have attained enlightenment like Guru Nanak, Ramana Maharshi or Gautam Buddha. In most cases, a Guru is required, as in the case of Saint Tukaram, Saint Gyaneshwar, or Saint Kabir. Some external 'body' acted as their guru. It is in rare cases that enlightenment is attained without a Guru. This is because the Truth can be revealed only when the mind surrenders completely. The mind, by itself, cannot make the mind surrender. You need to have a benevolent preceptor on whom you can have faith.

There are some who argue that a Guru is not needed and then there are some who spend all their time arguing that their Guru, their religion, and their portrayals of God are the correct ones. Because they are focused on the wrong thing, they never attain the Truth. To understand whether a Guru is required or not, it's first important to know who the Guru is.

Do you call a person Guru? Is it the body? No. Many people are caught up in this confusion. They have been told, "this particular person," or "this body" is your Guru. They are refrained from approaching anyone else or attending any other teachings. If they do so, they're considered disloyal. People lead their lives with this fear of being rejected.

Understand this. *A body is not a Guru. The Consciousness, which manifests through that body is the Guru. The Consciousness within*

you that is yet to be revealed is the Guru. It is that Consciousness that guides you. It may guide you through a person, a book, or dream. So what do you have to do? Just be open and receptive. Don't close yourself saying that if others can attain Self-realization on their own, then I can too. That's not in your hands. Just be open and let Consciousness guide you.

Attaining human life is the first grace. If the thirst to attain the ultimate truth of life arises within you, then that is the second grace. When the disciple is ready, the Guru has to appear. The appearance of the Guru in your life is the third grace. If you are able to develop unshakeable faith in the Guru, then this is the fourth grace. It is with God's grace that you receive a Guru. And it is with the grace of the Guru that you realize God. Ultimately, Guru, God, Grace and You are one and the same.

Seeker 1: What is the role of a Guru in the life of a seeker of Truth?

Sirshree: The word Guru is made up of two syllables 'Gu' and 'Ru,' meaning darkness and light. Guru means "One who dispels darkness." Darkness refers to ignorance, delusion, false beliefs.

A living Guru is important because he can guide you according to the nature of your body-mind mechanism. Therefore, you progress fast. When he sees you, he understands how far you've come and what your hurdles are. The teachings and the instructions delivered by the living Guru have a very deep impact. If you try to hit someone with a bullet held in your hand, the bullet won't have an impact. But the Guru is like a gun. When the bullet of wisdom is shot from the Guru, it hits the person with tremendous momentum and causes a deep transformation in his life. If the disciple listens to the Truth from someone who is not a true Guru, then the impact is like the bullet thrown from the hand. When the disciple listens to the same knowledge from the true Guru, his ego is eliminated.

The words delivered by the living Guru are very powerful because they are directly coming from the experience of the Self, from the very Source of Truth. Therefore, the disciples abide by his words with devotion and complete surrender.

The Guru kindles faith in the heart of the one who follows the path of wisdom, which leads the contrast mind to surrender completely. Such faith is essential for the doubting mind to be able to doubt itself; to doubt its own ideas and beliefs.

Seeker 1: How can a true Guru be recognized?

Sirshree: How do you identify your Guru? Your Guru is where your mind calms down and where its habit of vacillating in thoughts subsides. Your Guru is where you become free from deceit. If the mind's habit of vacillating in thoughts begins to diminish, you are at the right place. The true Guru will lead you towards the state that transcends thoughts. The true Guru dissolves your beliefs, your false notions. In fact, it is in the Guru's presence that the disciple starts transcending the mind and body. Once you are in contact with your Guru, your life is transformed.

The right Guru has the complete understanding of Self Experience, the state of Liberation, the state of Samadhi - the timeless state of pure beingness. The true Guru is the Self that is established in itself and able to guide you towards Self-realization. The One who has attained liberation alone can lead you to the final Truth.

Seeker 1: Thanks for this guidance. So what are the next steps for me to move towards Self-stabilization?

Sirshree: *The process of stabilizing in Self-experience involves the practice of Sadhana – the eradication of past conditioning of the mind through right understanding. You should remain in the company of Truth – be in the presence of of Truth through constant listening, contemplation and meditation.*

Develop the habit of shifting your focus from negativity, from that which is temporary, to that which is real and permanent. Practice this through the various incidents that unfold in daily life by conscious questioning. The mind is cleansed by uncovering the mechanical reactive patterns that are helplessly manifested through the body due to ignorance and lowered consciousness.

During this journey, it is possible that the mind may be frustrated at times, as it may not see results immediately forthcoming. The mind likes to see results instantly as per its own imaginations. *The mind returns again and again with various questions, doubts about the goal. This is where the role of a living Guru comes in to put all such doubts to rest and direct the seeker to transcend the mind. It is perseverance, faith and devotion that help in relentlessly continuing the pursuit.*

Seeker 2: Gratitude, Sirshree!

Sirshree: Thanks for giving this opportunity to serve you. Happy Thoughts!

About Sirshree

Sirshree's spiritual quest which began during his childhood, led him on a journey through various schools of thought and meditation practices. His overpowering desire to attain the truth made him relinquish his teaching job. After a long period of contemplation, his spiritual quest culminated in the attainment of the ultimate truth. Sirshree says, **"All paths that lead to the truth begin differently, but end in the same way—with understanding. Understanding is the whole thing. Listening to this understanding is enough to attain the truth."**

Sirshree is the author of several spiritual books. His books have been translated in more than 10 languages and published by leading publishers such as Penguin and Hay House. He is the founder of Tej Gyan Foundation, a not-for-profit organization committed to raising mass consciousness by spreading "Happy Thoughts" with branches in the United States, India, Europe and Asia-Pacific. Sirshree's retreats have transformed the lives of thousands and his teachings have inspired various social initiatives for raising global consciousness.

His works include more than 100 books and 3000 discourses. Various luminaries and celebrities such as His Holiness the Dalai Lama, publishers Mr. Reid Tracy and Ms. Tami Simon and yoga master Dr. B. K. S Iyengar have released Sirshree's books and lauded his work. 'The Source' book series, authored by Sirshree, has sold more than 10 million copies in 5 years. His book *The Warrior's Mirror*, published by Penguin, was featured in the Limca Book of Records for being released on the same day in 11 languages.

Tejgyan... The Road Ahead

What is Tejgyan?

Tejgyan is the existential wisdom of the ultimate truth, which is beyond duality. In today's world, there are people who feel disharmony and are desperately trying to achieve balance in an unpredictable life. Tejgyan helps them in harmonizing with their true nature, the Self, thereby restoring balance in all aspects of their life.

And then there are those who are successful but feel a sense of emptiness or void within. Tejgyan provides them fulfillment and helps them to embark on a journey towards self-realization. There are others who feel lost and are seeking the meaning of life. Tejgyan helps them to realize the true purpose of human life.

All this is possible with Tejgyan due to a very simple reason. The experience of the ultimate truth is always available. The direct experience of this truth is possible provided the right method is known. Tejgyan is that method, that understanding. At Tej Gyan Foundation, Sirshree imparts this understanding through a System for Wisdom – a series of retreats that guides participants step by step

Magic of Ultimate Awakening Retreat

Magic of Ultimate Awakening is the flagship self-realization retreat offered by Tej Gyan Foundation The retreat is conducted in two languages – Hindi and English. The teachings of the retreat are non-denominational (secular).

This residential retreat is held for 3-5 days at the foundation's MaNaN Ashram amidst the glory of mountains and the pristine beauty of nature. This ashram is located at the outskirts of the city of Pune in India, and is well connected by air, road and rail. The retreat is also held at other centres of Tej Gyan Foundation across the world.

Participate in the *Magic of Ultimate Awakening* retreat to attain ageless wisdom through a unique simple 'System for Wisdom' so that you can:

1. Live from pure and still presence allowing the natural qualities of consciousness, viz. peace, love, joy, compassion, abundance and creativity to manifest.

2. Acquire simple tools to use in everyday life which help quieten the chattering mind, revealing your true nature.

3. Get practical techniques to access pure presence at will and connect to the source of all answers (the inner guru).

4. Discover missing links in practices of meditation *(dhyana)*, action *(karma)*, wisdom *(gyana)* and devotion *(bhakti)*.

5. Understand the nature of your body-mind mechanism to attain freedom from tendencies and patterns.

6. Learn practical methods to shift from mind-centred living to consciousness-centred living.

For retreats contact +919921008060 or email: mail@tejgyan.com

About Tej Gyan Foundation

Tej Gyan Foundation (TGF) was established with the mission of creating a highly evolved society through all-round self development of every individual that transforms all the facets of his/her life. It is a non-profit organization founded on the teachings of Sirshree. The foundation has received the ISO certification (ISO 9001:2015) for its system of imparting wisdom. It has centres all across India as well as in other countries. The motto of Tej Gyan Foundation is 'Happy Thoughts'.

TGF is creating a highly evolved society through:

- Tejgyan Programs (Retreats, Courses, Television and Radio Programs, Podcasts)

- Tejgyan Products (Books, Tapes, Audio/Video CDs)

- Tejgyan Projects (Value Education, Women Empowerment, Peace Initiatives)

TGF undertakes projects to elevate the level of consciousness among students, youth, women, senior citizens, teachers, doctors, leaders, organizations, police force, prisoners, etc.

MaNaN Ashram

Survey No. 43, Sanas Nagar, Nandoshi gaon, Kirkatwadi Phata, Sinhagad Road, Dist. Pune 411024, Maharashtra, India.

Books can be delivered at your doorstep by registered post or courier. You can request for the same through postal money order or pay by VPP. Please send the money order to either of the following two addresses:

1. WOW Publishings Pvt. Ltd.
Registered Office: E-4, Vaibhav Nagar, Near Tapovan Mandir, Pimpri, Pune 411017.

2. Post Box No. 36, Pimpri Colony Post Office, Pimpri, , Pune 411017

Phone No. : 9011013210 / 9623457873

You can also order your copy at the online store:
www.gethappythoughts.org
Free Shipping plus 10% Discount on purchases above Rs. 300/-*

For further details contact:

Tejgyan Global Foundation

Registered Office:
Happy Thoughts Building, Vikrant Complex, Near
Tapovan Mandir, Pimpri, Pune 411017, Maharashtra, India.
Contact No: 020-27411240, 27412576
Email: mail@tejgyan.com

MaNaN Ashram:
Survey No. 43, Sanas Nagar, Nandoshi gaon, Kirkatwadi Phata,
Sinhagad Road, Tal. Haveli, Dist. Pune 411024, Maharashtra, India.
Contact No: 992100 8060.

Hyderabad: 9885558100, **Bangalore:** 9880412588,

Delhi: 9891059875, **Nashik:** 9326967980, **Mumbai:** 9373440985

For accessing our unique 'System for Wisdom' from self-help to self-realization, please follow us on:

	Website	www.tejgyan.org
You Tube	Video Channel	www.youtube.com/tejgyan For Q&A videos: http://goo.gl/YA81DQ
facebook	Social networking	www.facebook.com/tejgyan
twitter	Social networking	www.twitter.com/sirshree
	Internet Radio	http://www.tejgyan.org/internetradio.aspx

Online Shopping
www.gethappythoughts.org

Pray for World Peace along with thousands of others at 09:09 a.m. and p.m. every day

www.ingramcontent.com/pod-product-compliance
Lightning Source LLC
LaVergne TN
LVHW040157080526
838202LV00042B/3211